# NOT MY GIRL

Christy Jordan-Fenton & Margaret Pokiak-Fenton
Art by **Gabrielle Grimard**

**annick press**
toronto + berkeley

Margaret with her parents, around 1937

It was as though the wings of one thousand birds soared in my heart, propelling me back to my family. I leapt over the side of the boat and ran toward my mother.

Her face remained as still as stone.

"Not my girl!" she called in what
little English she knew. The birds
in my heart fell from their sky.

I caught a glint of my own reflection in my mother's hard eyes. The long braids she had once lovingly plaited had been cut away, along with everything she remembered of me.

I had grown tall and very thin from two years of hard chores and poor meals at the outsiders' school.

When I left for Aklavik, I was just eight. Now I was ten. In that time I had learned how to add numbers and how to read books. I had perfect table manners and knew when to say my prayers. I could speak English and French. But I no longer knew the words in my own language to tell my mother that I *was* her girl.

"Not my girl!" rang out again like the slap of a ruler on a desk.

I turned to my sisters and brother. They just stared.

I tensed to run, but my father caught me in a tight embrace.

"Olemaun," he whispered. I had not heard my Inuit name in so long I thought it might shatter like an eggshell with the weight of my father's voice. At the school I was known only by my Christian name, Margaret. I buried my head in my father's smoky parka, turning it wet with tears. I felt a touch much gentler than my father's strong grasp as my mother's arms joined his. Together they sheltered me in that safe place between them.

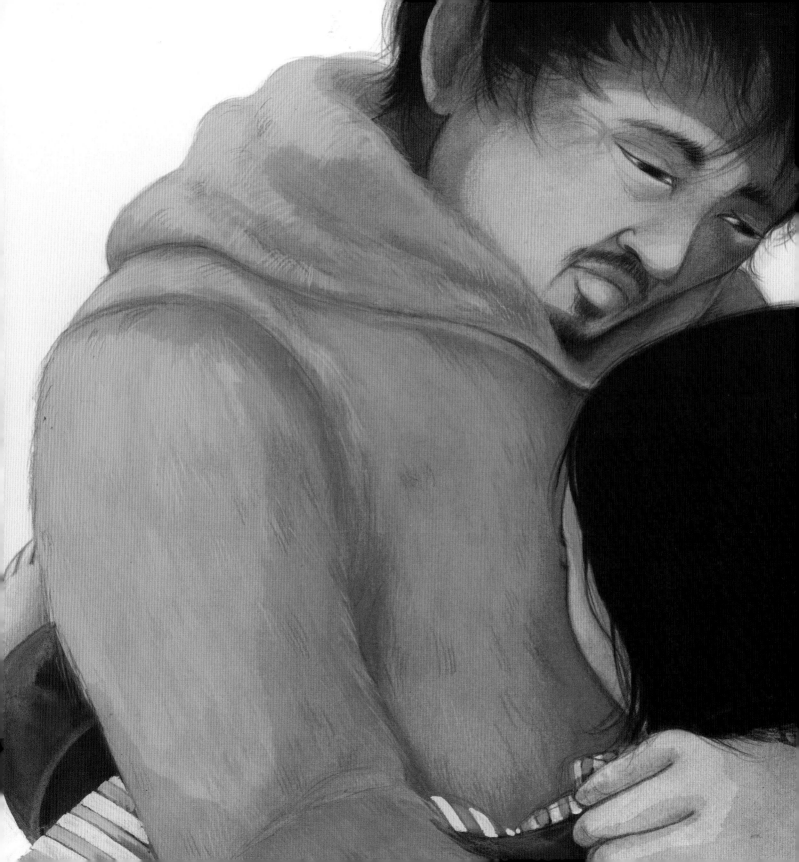

We might have embraced forever had my tummy not growled! Luckily, my mother had brought my favorite foods for me: whale blubber *muktuk* and dried fish *pipsi*. No more cabbage soup, porridge, or muskrat like I was fed at the school.

I took a piece of *muktuk*
and shoved it in my mouth.
I chewed and chewed it and
tried to wrestle the rubbery
chunk down. But my throat
closed and my stomach turned.

I had to spit it out.

I followed my family home
silently. As they honked
away like a gaggle of geese,
I wondered what kind of bird
I had become. I no longer felt
like I belonged to this flock.

As we neared our tent, I caught sight of my father's
sled dogs! I ran eagerly toward one, but she sprang
at me with a fierce snap.

"Wait until you wear our scent again, Olemaun,"
my father said, reassuring me with the English
he had learned as a boy at an outsiders' school.

My first few weeks at home were difficult. I could not
eat the food my mother prepared. I relied on my father
to translate almost everything. And I had lost the skills
I needed to be useful.

I couldn't set traps, skin hares, or pluck geese.
I knew how to recite verses and make my bed,
but those things did not help feed the family.
I wished my older sister had not moved away.
She had been to the outsiders' school.
She would have understood how hard
it was to return home a stranger.

One day, after I tangled a fishing net,
my mother gestured for me to go play.

I ran straight for my friend Agnes's house. She was my best friend from school and I wanted to see if she would like to go hunting for goose eggs— a food we both loved.

Her mother met me at the door with a stern look. Agnes joined her.

"My mother and father say I am an outsider now. They do not want me playing with children from the school," Agnes said timidly, before closing the door.

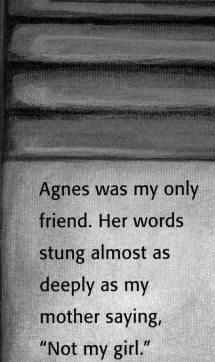

Agnes was my only friend. Her words stung almost as deeply as my mother saying, "Not my girl."

Dizzy with hunger and disappointment,
I stumbled home. A dog leapt up as
I approached. Wanting to know if I would
always be an outsider, I offered a hand.
The dog answered with a snarl and
a flash of sharp teeth that nearly took
off my fingers. I retreated to a corner of
the tent and hid in my favorite book until
my family returned.

My sisters had caught many
fish and I was jealous. Then
my mother placed her ulu
in my hands. She guided
the knife up the fish's belly,
patiently showing me how
to gut it.

That night as I reached for a piece of fish, I thought for a moment how embarrassed I would be if the nuns could see me eating with my hands. But I was proud that I had helped to prepare the fish and it had been a long while since we had a meal I could eat, so I gorged myself.

When the air turned crisp again, one of the dogs had a litter of pups. Agnes would love them! I had relearned many of the words of my people, so I decided to try to see her again. I carefully snatched a soft pup, belted it into the back of my parka like a baby, and set off.

My hand trembled as it struck her door. No one answered. After a long wait I gave up. I walked down to the beach, took out my puppy and played with it, and sang it songs I remembered from school.

Arriving home late for supper, I quickly stripped off my parka, forgetting the puppy. My father leapt and caught it just before it hit the floor.

"Olemaun!" my mother shouted.

As I looked at the nearly lifeless body,
I felt a searing of cold remorse.

"How long have you had this puppy?"
my father asked.

I shrugged. "Since morning."

My father knelt down. "Olemaun,
puppies need their mothers' milk."

"Will it die?" I asked.

"I'm not sure," he said sadly.

It was all too much. I turned and ran out into the night, where the iridescent fronds of the northern lights danced down from the sky. Grandmother once told me that if I whistled to them, their tendrils would reach down and snatch me away. I whistled until my lips hurt, but they ignored me.

Instead of scolding me when I returned, my father called me to the fire and handed me an eyedropper. I took it, sucked up some rice water, and released it into the puppy's mouth. I had nursed patients at the hospital next to the school and knew how to care for the sick. I stayed up all night feeding my little patient.

In the morning we took the puppy outside.
At first his mother pushed him away. He
whimpered. Like me, he no longer carried his
family's scent. I closed my eyes and wished
with all my heart I'd never taken him. When
I looked again, his mother was licking him.
My father squeezed me to him and smiled.

By the time the snows came, eating was
getting easier. And while I was still happy
to share my *muktuk* with the puppy, I kept
the *pipsi* for myself. I had regained my
family's scent, and often helped my father
with the dogs.

One day, he asked me to join him on a hunting trip. I was ecstatic! I loved traveling by dogsled.

We were far out on the barren tundra when my father asked, "Olemaun, do you know the dog commands?"

"Yes," I said confidently. "*Gee* means go right and left is *haw*."

He laughed, hopping off and leaving me in command. The dogs were moving fast and my heart was racing. "*Haw*," I called excitedly, meaning to avoid the pond on the left. But I had confused my commands. The dogs went toward the pond!

"*Gee! Gee!*" I shouted. The dogs bolted sharply right.

"*Haw! Haw!*" I countered. They darted so quickly left, I nearly flew off the sled. Panicked, I repeated "*Haw! Haw!*" My command tamed the line into a tight coil that slowed to a gradual stop.

"Atta girl, Olemaun!" my father shouted.

As we rode back to town, I felt proud standing ahead of him on the runners. I was sure he was proud too. He let me drive often after that.

On Christmas morning I awoke to the smell of bannock.
My father sat like Santa with a load of presents. He gave
my brother a train and my sisters beautiful porcelain dolls.
There was nothing for me.

I cried. I had tried
so hard, but I still
did not belong.

"What's wrong?"
my father asked.

"I wanted a doll,"
I sobbed.

"I thought you were too old for dolls," he teased.

"Maybe you are not big enough for your own dogsled."

"My own dogsled!"

I ran outside to find six
dogs hitched to a new sled.
I hopped on and drove
around and around town
beneath the dancing
northern lights. I passed
by Agnes and her mother.
At that speed I could not
see their expressions,
but they both waved
and cheered!

As I neared home I saw that my father had his own team of dogs hitched and my brother and sisters loaded on his sled. I slowed, allowing my mother to climb on the runners behind me, my eyelashes freezing with tears.

As we all sped off like a swift winged flock, the sound of my mother's voice filled my ears. "My girl!" she shouted proudly, and the birds rose up in my heart to soar high once again.

## Dedications

For my three little
Inspirations. And for
Marty Simon and
Debra Grant, two
beautiful souls who
have each created
safe places for healing
—Christy

For all the children
still trying to find their
way home. May you
each discover a way
to step out from the
darkness behind you
into the light ahead
—Margaret

For my children
—Gabrielle

© 2014 Christy Jordan-Fenton and Margaret Pokiak-Fenton (text)
© 2014 Gabrielle Grimard (illustrations)

Fifth printing, August 2017

Edited by Debbie Rogosin
Designed by Natalie Olsen/Kisscut Design

Annick Press Ltd.

We acknowledge the support of the Canada Council for the Arts, the Ontario Arts Council, and the participation of the Government of Canada/la participation du gouvernement du Canada for our publishing activities.

Canadä | ONTARIO ARTS COUNCIL
CONSEIL DES ARTS DE L'ONTARIO
an Ontario government agency
un organisme du gouvernement de l'Ontario

### Cataloging in Publication

Jordan-Fenton, Christy, author
Not my girl / Christy Jordan-Fenton & Margaret Pokiak-Fenton ;
art by Gabrielle Grimard.

Previously published as: A stranger at home.
ISBN 978-1-55451-625-4 (bound).—ISBN 978-1-55451-624-7 (pbk.)

1. Pokiak-Fenton, Margaret—Childhood and youth—Juvenile literature. 2. Inuit—Canada—Residential schools—Juvenile literature. 3. Inuit—Cultural assimilation—Canada—Juvenile literature. 4. Inuit women—Biography—Juvenile literature. I. Pokiak-Fenton, Margaret, author II. Grimard, Gabrielle, 1975–, artist III.Jordan-Fenton, Christy. Stranger at home. IV. Title.

E96.5.J652 2014          j371.829'9712071          C2013-906425-7

Published in the U.S.A. by Annick Press (U.S.) Ltd.
Distributed in Canada by University of Toronto Press.
Distributed in the U.S.A. by Publishers Group West.

Printed in China

Also available in e-book format.
Please visit **www.annickpress.com/ebooks.html**
for more details. Or scan